Y0-AQN-462

Ruby Red Shoes

KATE KNAPP

📖 Angus&Robertson
An imprint of HarperCollins*Children'sBooks*

Angus & Robertson

An imprint of HarperCollins*Children'sBooks*, Australia

First published in Australia in 2012
by HarperCollins*Publishers* Australia Pty Limited
ABN 36 009 913 517
harpercollins.com.au

HarperCollins*Publishers*
Level 13, 201 Elizabeth Street, Sydney, NSW 2000, Australia
Unit D1, 63 Apollo Drive, Rosedale, Auckland 0632, New Zealand
A 53, Sector 57, Noida, UP, India
1 London Bridge Street, London, SE1 9GF, United Kingdom
2 Bloor Street East, 20th floor, Toronto, Ontario M4W 1A8, Canada
195 Broadway, New York NY 10007, USA

National Library of Australia Cataloguing-in-Publication entry

Knapp, Kate.
    Ruby red shoes / Kate Knapp.
    9780732293628 (hbk.)
    For primary school age.
    Children's stories.

A823.4

Cover and internal design by Natalie Winter
The illustrations in this book were created in pencil and watercolour
Colour reproduction by Graphic Print Group, Adelaide
Printed and bound in China by RR Donnelley on 180g Goldsun Woodfree

27 26 25 24   17 18 19 20

For my wonderful parents
Cynthia and Patrick

Ruby Red Shoes is a white hare.

Ruby Red Shoes was given her name when she
was a baby. Her tiny feet would get as cold
as river pebbles, so her kindly grandmother
knitted her a pair of red shoes.

They were the colour of radishes
and when anyone tried to take them
off her feet, she would squeal.

Since then Ruby has always worn red shoes.

Ruby Red Shoes lives with her grandmother
in a prettily painted caravan.

Her grandmother's name
is Babushka Galina Galushka.

'Babushka' means 'grandmother',
'Galina' means 'calm'
and 'Galushka' means 'dumpling'.

She is soft and cuddly,
and smells of violets, which are
her favourite flowers.

Babushka Galushka encourages Ruby to be
an *aware* hare, treating everyone's feelings,
as well as her own, with great care.

'Feelings are just like delicate birds' eggs,' she would say.
'Be as gentle as you can with them.'

She also showed Ruby how to talk with all
animals, plants and trees and to respect every
living thing's important place on this earth.

The colourful caravan
is warm and cosy, and friends
are always welcome.

It is filled with all the things that Ruby
and Babushka Galushka love.

There are generous teacups for hot drinks,
feathery quilts to snuggle up in,
jars of colourful buttons
and posies of flowers in pots and jugs.

There are soft, warm chairs
and places to drift off and snooze.

One of Ruby's most cherished places is
the glorious deep bath. It sits on grand
feet shaped like a lion's paws.

Sometimes when Ruby is submerged
up to her chin, she imagines the bath may suddenly
decide it's tired of standing still and run off into
the forest with her bobbing along inside.

It sounds an exciting adventure
until she begins to feel seasick!

Much of Ruby's day is
spent in her garden.

She loves gardening and grows all her own vegetables, fruit, herbs and flowers.

There are always so many things to do
in the garden — seedlings to be planted and watered,
busy, buzzy bees to be calmed with gentle words.

All the while, Ruby sings sweet songs
to everything that grows.

The garden is filled with delicious food to eat.

Green peas — best eaten straight
from the pod.

Sweet, happy mint.

Crunchy carrots – cut into
twigs for snacking.

Ravishing radishes.

Blushing peaches.

Mulberries — for making little hands
a pretty berry colour.

Ruby's wonderful garden is home
to a jazzy group of chickens.

Ruby gives the chickens all the things
they need to be happy — a safe and
comfortable home and a menu of tasty
and nourishing food to nibble.

To keep them fabulously fit,
Ruby teaches the ladies to play soccer
— with a passionfruit.
They cheat dreadfully!

Ruby's chickens are curious and clever.
They love to learn, so Ruby teaches them
French, which they adore.

But they now ask for baguettes
and croissants instead of ordinary
breadcrumbs!

Ruby also loves the peace and
stillness in her garden.

The floating butterflies,

dancing green leaves

and whispering trees are perfect
for soothing an aware hare.

Ruby enjoys little naps in the cool grass.
Often she daydreams, watching the breeze tickling
the leaves or hurrying lazy clouds through
the powdery-blue sky.

The washing line makes happy
snapping noises as the billowy linen
tries to fly away with the wind.

After such a busy day in the garden,
Ruby welcomes bedtime, when Babushka
Galushka tucks her under her cosy quilt.

Together they look out to the marvellous,
velvety night sky and thank the millions upon
millions of magical twinkling stars staying up all
night to watch over their happy caravan.

Natalie McComas

Illustrator and artist Kate Knapp is a graduate of the Queensland College of Art. Her design studio, Twigseeds, produces cards, prints, stationery and books.

Ruby Red Shoes was shortlisted for the 2013 Children's Book Council of Australia Crichton Award for Children's Book Illustration.

Kate's second book, *Ruby Red Shoes Goes to Paris*, was shortlisted for the 2014 Australian Book Industry Award for Book of the Year for Younger Children and for the 2014 Inaugural Readings Children's Book Prize.

Visit Ruby at www.rubyredshoes.com.au

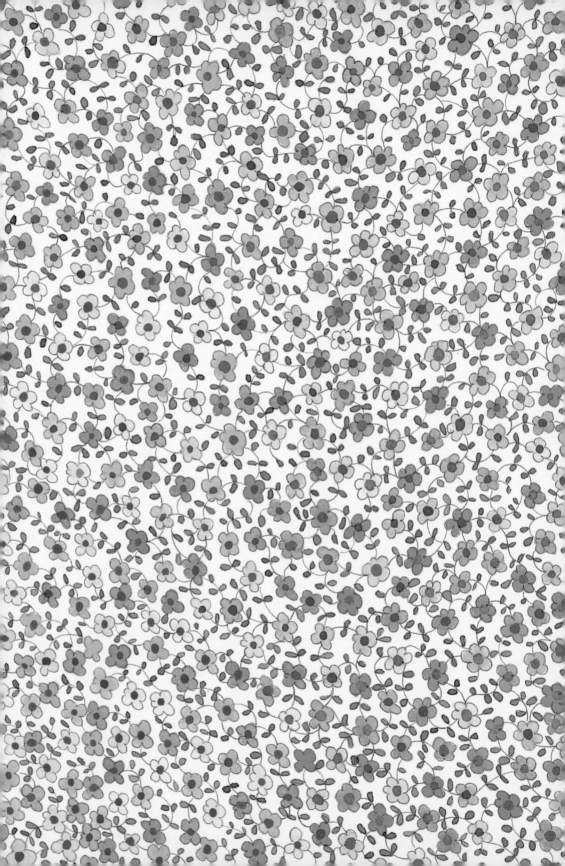